The Knighting of Sir Sticky Von Bear

Gabriel & Kelly Shields

Illustrated by Zemeira Walker

 Narrabbit Books

NARRABBIT BOOKS

Narrabbit Books started as nothing more than a hidden character in a comic that Gabriel started in college. Soon, readers followed the narrabbit's adventures all around the world as Kelly would take him on her international business trips. Although he took a little break from his travels, he's back and ready to bring fun, whimsical, Christ-centered children's books to families. Sticky Bear is just the first character introduced by Narrabit Books, there are many more to come! Follow the narrabbit and see what you find at narrabbit.com

Cover Design and Book Layout by Kelly Shields

Music notes by rawpixel.com / Freepik

Author photo taken by Izabela Mattson Photography

Narrabbit Books

Albany, OR

narrabbit.com

Print ISBN: 979-8-9895543-0-0

For our very own little sticky bear

G.S. & K.S.

For Aspen, Esther, Orion, and Timmy

Z.W.

Once there was a bear who was ever so sticky. He had always been sticky. He was born sticky. And being sticky is just no fun at all!

This would get stuck to him. That would get stuck to him. And everyone would tease him and call him Sticky Bear.

As he passed through the town they would poke fun at him, singing

Why are you ever so sticky?

You're a little bear that's sticky icky.

Forgive me if I sound a bit picky.

But you're a little sticky bear.

Poor little bear. It seemed everything stuck to him, even the name "Sticky."

Try as he might, he could not get them to call him by his real name. Fed up, one day he announced, "If I'm to be Sticky Bear then I shall be Sir Sticky Von Bear, the greatest knight in all the land!" For what could be better than to be a knight?

But as sticky as he was, this seemed to be the one thing that just wouldn't stick.

So he proclaimed, "I will make it stick! I'm Sticky Von Bear after all!" and he set off to find a kingdom where he could become a knight.

On his way, he passed a small stone cottage where he thought he heard a voice call his name. "Couldn't be," Sticky thought. "No one ever calls me by my real name." So he continued along.

A little further he came across a very wealthy kingdom, the wealthiest kingdom in all the land. There were trinkets, treasures, and toys as far as the eye could see.

"Now this is a kingdom worthy of a knight!" Sticky thought to himself.

But Sticky knew he couldn't go before a king looking the way he did. So he scrubbed his paws and combed the tangles, removed the twigs and shook out the leaves, until he was the kind of clean fit for a king. But by the time he reached the palace, he was once again just as sticky as before.

The trumpets blasted to announce the king as he took his seat.

"What do we have here?" asked the king as he weighed his gold on the royal scales.

"A knight!" Sticky replied.

"My kingdom is full of treasure, but I want more. There is a great dragon whose scales can make copies of any treasure. Bring me one and you'll prove you're worthy to be a knight of my kingdom."

"I won't fail you!" said Sticky as he went off to retrieve it.

He set out and found the dragon sleeping. What luck!

Sticky was able to grab one of the scales, but the dragon awoke and began chasing him. What a sticky situation!

Luckily for the little bear, he'd left a puddle of stickiness and the dragon was stuck in his tracks.

Sticky returned and everyone cheered!

But when he tried to hand over the scale, he found he just couldn't let go. It was stuck to him just like everything else.

The king summoned his men to pull with all their might until the scale came loose.

The king was ecstatic and was just about to make Sticky a knight, but to the king's dismay every piece of treasure he copied using the dragon's scale came out sticky.

"Look what you've done! Our stuff is valuable, but you've ruined it!"

Why are you ever so sticky?
You're a little bear that's sticky icky.
Forgive me if I sound a bit picky.
But you're a little sticky bear.

The king said unamused as he sent Sticky away. Feeling discouraged, Sticky Bear went off to find another kingdom, still hopeful he could become a knight.

Once again he passed by the familiar small stone cottage. Again he thought he heard a voice call his real name.

   This time he stopped. Gazing up at the window he thought he saw someone looking right at him. Even though Sticky was the only one there, he still thought, "I must be imagining things, no one would ever call for me." So he hurried along, eager to find the next kingdom.

Soon he came across a kingdom full of very wise people, the wisest in all the land. Here everyone always had the answer and they loved to debate each other to show just how smart they really were.

"Now this is a kingdom worthy of a knight!" Sticky thought to himself.

But Sticky knew he couldn't go before a king looking the way he did. So once again he scrubbed his paws and combed the tangles, removed the twigs and shook out the leaves, until he was the kind of clean fit for a king. But by the time he reached the palace, he was once again just as sticky as before.

The trumpets blasted to announce the king as he took his seat.

"What do we have here?" asked the king as he peered up from his seeing stone.

"A knight!" Sticky replied.

"My kingdom is full of wisdom, but I want more. There is a Great Sphinx who knows the answer to everything and guards the fruit of knowledge. Bring me the fruit by asking her an unsolvable question and you'll prove you're worthy to be a knight of my kingdom."

"I won't fail you!" said Sticky as he went off to retrieve the fruit of knowledge.

Sticky set out and found the Great Sphinx who told him to ask her an unsolvable question. Sticky thought for a moment.

Finally he asked her, "Why am I ever so sticky?" The Sphinx was stuck! Unable to answer, she rewarded Sticky with the fruit.

Sticky returned and everyone cheered!

But when he tried to hand over the fruit, he found he just couldn't let go. It was stuck to him just like everything else.

The king summoned his men to pull with all their might until the fruit came loose.

The king was ecstatic and was just about to make Sticky a knight, but to the king's dismay every time he took a bite his thoughts stuck together so he couldn't tell this from that.

"You can't learn how to be unsticky. As sticky as you are I'm surprised this concept hasn't stuck in your mind!"

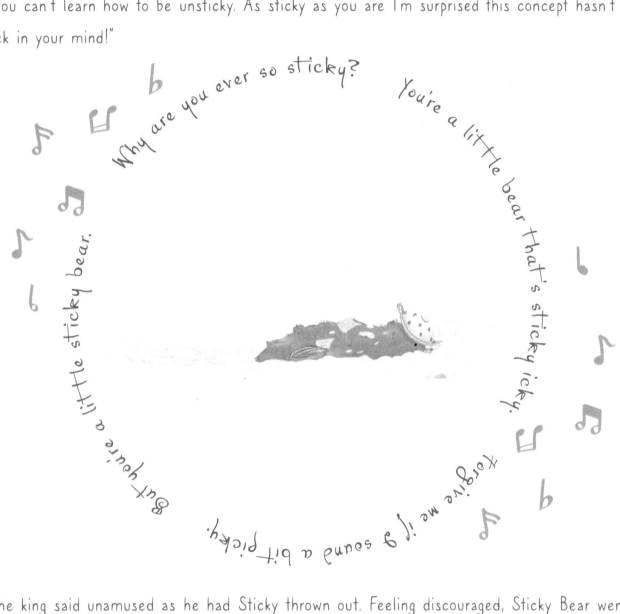

Why are you ever so sticky? You're a little bear that's sticky icky. Forgive me if g sound a bit picky. But you're a little sticky bear.

The king said unamused as he had Sticky thrown out. Feeling discouraged, Sticky Bear went off to find another kingdom, still hopeful he could become a knight.

Once more he passed by the familiar cottage. Again he thought he heard a voice call his name.

This time when he stopped and looked there was no doubt that someone was indeed calling for him, but still he thought, "Well, I'm not imagining it, but why would anyone be calling for me? I'm not a knight yet." So he continued on, determined to make a name for himself.

This time he came across a very beautiful kingdom, the most beautiful in all the land. Here everyone and everything looked as clean and pure as could be.

"Now this is a kingdom worthy of a knight!" Sticky thought to himself.

But Sticky knew he couldn't go before a king looking the way he did. This was his last chance. He scrubbed his paws and combed the tangles, removed the twigs and shook out the leaves. He even cleaned behind his ears; he washed himself until he was the kind of clean fit for a king. But by the time he reached the palace, he was once again just as sticky as before.

The trumpets blasted to announce the king as he took his seat.

"What do we have here?" asked the king as he primped and preened himself.

"A knight!" Sticky replied.

"My kingdom is full of beauty, but I want more. Eventually beauty fades, but there's a fountain with cleansing water that will make me youthful and beautiful forever. It's hidden away in an enchanted garden. Bring me some water and you'll prove you're worthy to be a knight of my kingdom."

"I won't fail you!" said Sticky as he went off to retrieve the cleansing water.

Sticky set out and found the fountain. But as he passed through the enchanted garden a giant plant gobbled him up.

Luckily for Sticky he got stuck in its throat. The plant didn't enjoy that very much so it hacked and it heaved until finally it spat Sticky out right in front of the fountain.

Sticky filled a bottle, and then stared into the water. If this water is so pure perhaps it could make him unsticky.

"This could be it!" thought Sticky as he dove into the fountain. And sure enough, when he climbed out, he appeared to be unsticky.

Sticky returned and everyone cheered!

But when he tried to hand over the bottle, to his surprise, he found he still just couldn't let go. It was stuck to him just like everything else.

The king summoned his men to pull with all their might until the bottle came loose.

The king was ecstatic and was just about to make Sticky a knight, but to the king's dismay every time he tried to open the lid, it was stuck to the bottle.

"Take a good look at yourself, Sticky, you'll never be good enough for any kingdom!" And all the people of the palace began to chant:

Why are you ever so sticky? You're a little bear that's sticky icky. Forgive me if I sound a bit picky. But you're a little sticky bear.

Sticky saw his reflection in the king's eyes and realized how ridiculous he looked.

Ashamed he ran away. Into the forest he went, crying as he ran. Even his tears stuck to his cheeks. Everyone would know that he was a sobbing, sticky failure. Sticky Bear felt hopeless.

"I'll never be a knight, I'm no good."

Sticky started the long journey back home. As he passed by the humble cottage once more, he stopped and took a long look at it; he had nowhere else to go. Again, he heard the same voice calling out to him. There was no doubt, he knew he was being called.

This time, Sticky responded. "What do you want from me?" he asked from the road.

"I want you to join me. I'm looking for a knight for my kingdom," replied the man.

"Oh no," sighed Sticky. "You wouldn't want me."

"Why wouldn't I want you? I've called you many times before."

"I'm much too sticky and will mess everything up, I'll fail you..." Sticky replied.

"What if I make you unsticky?"

"How can you? I've tried everything. Now I'm convinced that all the wealth in the world cannot fix my stickiness; all the wisdom in the world cannot understand my stickiness, and all the beauty in the world cannot cover up my stickiness. I'm nothing more than a sticky bear." Poor little bear sighed a deep sigh.

"Come and see. If you'll be a knight just as you are, I will make you clean."

Sticky looked at the man. There were no trumpets, no royal scales, no seeing stones, no primping or preening, just an honest man that seemed to actually want Sticky in his courts. With a flutter in his heart, Sticky walked up the cottage path.

The man asked Sticky to kneel and dubbed him as a knight, then presented him with glorious heavenly armor. As the little bear arose he was expecting to stick to the floor, but lo and behold, he did not stick! He was truly clean!

As he looked up he saw that the humble cottage had transformed into a magnificent palace and the humble man into a glorious king, the most glorious king of all.

The little bear was no longer sticky, but in his heart he knew that this was a king worth sticking with.

Now, if you were to come across this little bear on one of his many adventures, you'd hear him singing cheerfully:

I once was a bear who was ever so sticky.

I was a little bear who was sticky icky.

Forgive me for being so picky.

I'm no longer a sticky bear!

Hello Brave Knight,

Imagine it's your birthday--you've invited all your friends, you can't wait for them to come, and you hope everyone has a good time. But what if one of your friends is mean or tries to steal one of your gifts? You'd probably ask them to leave.

God has invited us all to the most amazing party ever--Heaven. Exciting, huh? However, anyone who has ever lied, stolen, said, or even thought something mean can't come. Have you ever done something like that? Everyone has.

Sadly, our hearts have a condition that keeps us from loving others perfectly--it's called sin. Nothing on earth can cure it. So if none of us are good enough for the party, who could possibly come?

Here's the good news! God loves you so much He couldn't imagine this party without you so He made a way despite all the bad things you've done. It isn't being good that gets us in, it's being forgiven. God sent His

son Jesus, who had a perfect heart without sin to die on a cross for the forgiveness of your sins. Jesus took your sin away and in exchange gave you a new heart that can enter Heaven.

Want to go to the party? Romans 10:9 tells us that all we have to do is say out loud what we believe in our hearts--that God raised Jesus from the dead for our sins.

In life you might put on a costume, like Sticky, that makes you look like a knight so others will accept and love you, but only Jesus can give you the real armor and offer you true love for who you are instead of what you do.

If you believe in Him then you've become a knight in God's kingdom. His knights invite others to His party and tell them about Jesus so they can come too.

Are you ready to start your new adventure, brave knight?

Gabriel and Kelly Shields share a love for fairy tales and children's books, and now that they're proud parents, they've found their lives (and shelves) filled with them. They hope to fill other family's bookshelves with stories that feed their souls and lead them to a deeper understanding of their identity and purpose in Christ. This is their very first children's book.

Discover more at narrabbit.com.

Zemeira Walker has been drawing since she could wield a crayon. She holds a Bachelors of the Arts in Communications, is continuing her education abroad in Theology and the Arts, and hopes to continue a career in illustration. The majority of her published pieces are digital, but her favorite mediums are ink and watercolor which inspires her freehanded digital style.

See more of her work at zemeirawalker.myportfolio.com.

Milton Keynes UK
Ingram Content Group UK Ltd.
UKHW051121011223
433600UK00004B/42